Lucia's Light

A Christmas story by Ashley Herzog

With Catherine Bristow

Chapter One

Karolina bounded out the front door of her family's house, hearing crisp fall leaves crunch under her boots. She was late for school. Most days, Karolina loved school. But she didn't like explaining to her teacher, Miss Donahoe, why she was late.

"Wait for me!" Karolina's little sister, Sofia, called behind her. Sofia was seven, two years younger than Karolina.

They walked the path that led to the heart of Manitonka, Wisconsin, the small city where they lived. It wasn't a great sprawling city, like Chicago or Milwaukee. But it was a city all the same. It had a Town Hall, a post office, five saloons, five churches—and, most important to Karolina and the other children of Manitonka, a schoolhouse. A short distance ahead, she could see the other students scurrying for the door before Miss Donahoe rang the schoolbell.

When Karolina stepped inside, she noticed the extra benches inside the schoolhouse, brand-new but empty.

"Miss Donahoe," Sofia said, talking out of turn, "Why are there more seats than yesterday?"

Miss Donahoe waited until all the children had taken their seats. Then, she explained.

"Good morning, boys and girls," she said, standing at the front of the room with her hands on her hips. "Tomorrow, you will have several new classmates."

The room buzzed with excitement.

"You must help them, and show patience," Miss Donahoe continued. "They are beginning to learn English. The children arrived a few months ago from Italy. Their families were recruited to work on the new railroad going North."

Karolina straightened up in her chair, excited about the news.

"When my Mama and Papa come to Manitonka, they didn't speak English," Karolina volunteered. "We came from Sweden. But I was only three years old, so I don't remember it well. Sofia was born on the steamboat we took to Wisconsin!"

Sofia's ears pricked. "That's right. I'm an American!" she declared with pride. "I was born here."

"Yes, we are all American," Miss Donahoe said. "But many of our parents and grandparents came from other places."

Miss Donahoe offered Karolina a slight smile as she passed her bench.

"I know you'll help the new children feel welcome in Manitonka, Karolina," she said. Karolina smiled back at her schoolteacher, feeling flutters of excitement in her belly.

As Karolina and Sofia walked home from school, they passed the big red house on Oak Street. Karolina had heard it was a boarding house. The new families in town lived there before they saved enough money for lumber to build their own houses. Today, there were horse-drawn wagons in front of the big house. The wagons held stacks of small trunks and burlap sacks.

Karolina spotted a girl about her age standing near one of the wagons. They locked eyes, and the girl gave Karolina a shy smile. Karolina smiled, too.

Suddenly, a round object whizzed through the air. It struck one of the wagons and bounced onto the brown autumn grass, rolling between a horse's front hooves.

"Go home, Papists!" an angry voice yelled. "Go home, foreigners! You're not welcome here!"

A woman wearing a shawl over her head gasped and grabbed the little girl's

hand. She rushed her inside. That was the last glimpse Karolina saw of her, her smile wiped away in an instant.

Karolina arrived home from the schoolhouse around the same time her older brother, Johan, came home from work. Johan was old enough to have completed school already, so he worked on a farm outside of town with Papa. Mama was home, too. Mama brought home extra money by working as a housemaid for Mayor Wisegarver. Mayor Wisegarver owned a beautiful mansion at the center of town. Every resident of Manitonka knew and respected their mayor. And Mama was lucky to have work cleaning his house.

"We are getting new classmates at school," Karolina told Mama and Johan. She was still excited despite what she had seen at the boarding house.

Mama was holding the youngest of the Henriksson siblings, baby Erik. She smiled. But behind her smile, she looked a little worried.

"I know, Karolina," she said. "And you must be kind to them, and help them learn their ABCs and to practice English. People were kind to us and the other Swedish families when we arrived in Manitonka."

There were many Swedish people in Manitonka. Years ago, before Karolina was born, brave Swedish families had set out for America. When the soil in Sweden became tired and overworked, they left to become farmers in the Great North—Wisconsin and Minnesota.

They made enough money to establish their own homesteads, and they wrote "America Letters" to their relatives in Sweden. They invited them to join them across the sea. In America, the farmland was rich, and new cities full of good jobs were springing up across the frontier.

The Henrikssons were one of the families that made the journey. Karolina was only three when they left Sweden. Mama and Papa and Johan, the oldest child, remembered it better.

"I will welcome them!" Karolina said. "I promise."

Before she went to sleep that night, she slipped her doll, Helmi, into her apron pocket. She was still thinking about the little girl with the dark hair she had seen outside the boarding house.

Chapter Two

"Good morning, boys and girls," Miss Donahoe said again the next morning. It was cold outside, and a light dusting of snow had fallen the night before, leaving a white shimmer on the grass outside the schoolhouse windows. The potbelly stove in the center of the room kept it warm, but Karolina was still cold. She took her seat next to Anna, whose parents had come from Sweden, too.

"Look at the new pupils," Anna said to Karolina, snickering a little. "They dress funny, don't they?"

Karolina looked to the back of the room, where a dozen boys and girls of different ages stood against the wall, looking shy and nervous. Most of them had dark hair and dark eyes. They looked much different than Karolina and Sofia, as well as Anna, who all had hair the color of summer wheat.

Karolina's eyes fell on the girl in the red cloak. There she was! The girl she had seen outside the boarding house yesterday afternoon. She thought of waving, but she didn't want Miss Donahoe to scold her for talking out of turn.

"Students, please meet our new pupils," Miss Donahoe said. She raised her chin and addressed the dark-haired children who stood against the wall. "Please come forward and state your names."

The new students buzzed among themselves, and one seemed to relay Miss Donahoe's message to the others. One by one, they approached the front of the room.

An older boy, nearly a teenager, went first.

"Angelo Mastromarino," he said. But his voice sounded different from the other students', and the name came out sounding foreign and strange. Some of the students giggled.

"Stella Argentieri," a girl, who looked about twelve, said.

"Their names are so strange and long," Anna whispered to Carolina. "How could we possibly remember them?"

Then, the girl from the boarding house approached the front of the room.

"Natalia," she whispered softly, and said no more.

Natalia. Now that was a name Karolina could remember!

At midday, Miss Donahoe excused the schoolhouse for recess. Anna stayed behind for help with one of her reading lessons. Karolina watched Natalia step cautiously out of the schoolhouse. She tapped her on the shoulder.

"Would you like to play with me and my doll, Helmi?" Karolina asked, holding up her beloved doll.

Natalia's brown eyes grew round, and her cheeks glowed. But she blinked at Karolina. She had not understood what she was saying.

"Play," Karolina repeated again, and Natalia nodded.

They sat under Karolina and Sofia's favorite oak tree, where they often played dolls at recess. Karolina offered Helmi to Natalia, who sat Helmi on her lap, examining her pretty, painted face.

"Where do you come from?" Karolina asked. She knew Natalia didn't speak English. But it didn't hurt to try.

Natalia's eyes sparkled, and Karolina knew that she somehow understood what she was saying. Natalia reached for a sturdy twig on the ground and began to draw a picture in the soft mud.

Karolina watched as she etched a shape into the earth. It looked like a lady's boot, with a slight heel and a pointed toe. Natalia used the stick to write "Italia" beside it.

"Yes, you're from Italy!" Karolina exclaimed. Natalia nodded and pointed to the ground. Near the toe of the boot, she drew a little misshapen rectangle. She etched the word "Sicilia" into the ground.

"Is that where you're from?" Karolina asked. Natalia nodded. Karolina picked up her own stick and drew the shape of Sweden, which she always thought looked like a long, malformed potato. Off the coast, she drew a little ship with sails, indicating that she, too, had sailed across the sea.

Natalia nodded. "Boat," she said.

Karolina's heart fluttered. They were communicating! They spoke two different languages, but they were talking all the same.

As Miss Donahoe rang the bell, signaling the students to return to the schoolhouse, Natalia slipped her hand into Karolina's.

More snow fell on Manitonka as autumn turned to winter. It was December now, and the schoolhouse was cold in the mornings before the stove got warm. Every day, Karolina invited Natalia to sit next to her and share her schoolbooks. They practiced writing English words. Even Anna, Karolina's friend who was also Swedish, had grown to welcome Natalia as a new friend.

Even if they couldn't communicate very well—yet.

"Good morning, boys and girls," Miss Donahoe said one December morning. "Today, we're going to talk about Christmas."

She walked between the rows of students, boys on one side, girls on the other. "People have different ways of celebrating Christmas in all the countries of the world. My own mother and father were born in Ireland. In Ireland, they have a tradition called mummering. Irish men and women dress up in elaborate costumes made from whatever material they can gather. Straw, old sheets, and the like. The mummers go house to house at Christmastime, demanding whisky and gin and sweet treats. They then performed the story of Irish heroes, like Brian Boru and King Connor of Ulster. Sometimes, they'd sit at the family's kitchen table and play games of dice in silence!"

The students laughed at the silly picture forming in their heads. How odd to play dice at a stranger's table in silence!

Miss Donahoe put her hands on her hips. "Like me, many of your mothers and fathers were born in different countries. In Manitonka, many of our townspeople came from Sweden. Some of you were even born there yourselves, like our Karolina." Karolina smiled at her teacher, and she smiled back.

"And now we have new students who come from Italy," Miss Donahoe said. "Tomorrow, I want you to be prepared to tell your schoolmates about Christmas traditions at home, where your family came from."

"My family celebrates St. Lucia Day," Anna said excitedly. "It's a special day in Sweden…"

Miss Donahoe put her hand up. "Save it for tomorrow morning, Anna," she said. "You may tell your schoolmates all about St. Lucia Day when the time comes."

As Miss Donahoe dismissed them for recess, Natalia tugged at Karolina's sleeve.

"Lucia," she said.

"Yes, Swedish people celebrate Lucia Day," Anna said, as the three of them walked outside. "My family celebrates it every year."

"My family does not," Karolina said with a sigh. "When we got to Wisconsin, my Papa thought it best to celebrate Christmas like the Americans."

She faintly remembered her last St. Lucia Day celebration, when she was a toddler in Sweden. She remembered the girl in a white gown carrying a tray of buns, a glowing crown of candles about her head…

Natalia shook her head. Anna and Karolina watched as she wound a piece of white yarn from her mittens into a ball. Then, she pointed to her eyes.

"Lucia," she said, motioning between her eyes and the ball of white yarn. She was trying to tell them something, but Karolina couldn't decipher it. She turned to Anna, who shrugged.

"I hope she learns English fast!" she said.

Karolina hoped so, too. Having a new friend was nice, but being able to talk to her would be wonderful.

"Friend," she said in halting English, smiling at her.

"Yes," Karolina replied. "We'll be the best of friends!"

Chapter Three

"Mayor Wisegarver called an urgent Town Hall meeting tonight."

Karolina overheard her parents talking in the kitchen. She was in the loft of their small, cozy home, where she shared a bed with Anna. Her older brother Johan's bed was on the other side of the room.

"I spend enough time listening to Mr. Wisegarver and his ideas," Mama said, sounding irritated. "I don't need to hear more."

"If we miss the meeting, our neighbors will wonder why," Papa argued. "We should at least go, and hear what the Mayor has to say. It's about the foreigners."

Foreigners. Karolina thought of Natalia and the other new children at school. Was that why Mayor Wisegarver was calling a Town Hall meeting? It was hard to believe the mayor of Manitonka wanted to call a meeting about schoolchildren. Shouldn't he tend to grown-up things?

"We were foreigners in this land once," Mama reminded him. Karolina heard the long pause between them.

"I know, Dagmar," Papa replied. "But men on the farm say they've come to take our jobs! For now, they work on the railroad. But what happens when they want other jobs in Manitonka?"

"Perhaps our city will grow. Maybe Manitonka will boom, like Milwaukee and Chicago," Mama replied.

Karolina peered over the edge of the loft. She watched Mama stir the kettle on the stove while holding baby Erik. "I will go with you," she said. "But we don't have to march in lockstep with Mayor Wisegarver and his friends."

After supper, Mama and Papa left for the meeting. Mama carried baby Erik with her.

"Read your schoolbooks and prepare for your lessons tomorrow," Mama said to Karolina and Sofia. "We will be back after you are in bed."

"Yes, Mama," Karolina said. But as soon as the door closed behind them, she turned to Johan and Sofia.

"We should follow them!" she whispered, in case Mama and Papa were still within earshot.

"Follow them? Why?" Johan asked, his blue eyes round with worry.

"Mayor Wisegarver is having a meeting about 'foreigners,'" Karolina said. She stumbled over the unfamiliar word. "Some people in Manitonka are angry about the Italians who came to work on the railroad.

But they go to school with us, and besides not knowing English, they're schoolchildren— just like us."

"The men are afraid they'll take our jobs," Johan said. "The Swedish men in Manitonka worked hard to get the better jobs on the farms and in the city. We can't go back to being small-time family farmers!"

"Mama says that when a city has more workers, it grows," Karolina said. She recalled the conversation she overheard earlier in the evening.

Sofia clasped her hands together. "It would be great fun to sneak into the Town Hall!" she cried.

The Henriksson siblings slipped into their boots and jackets, carefully locking the door behind them. And then they tiptoed out to the grand hall in the center of town.

Manitonka residents packed the rows of seats. Johan, Karolina, and Sofia crouched in the back of the room, behind the last row, where they hoped no one would see them.

Mayor Wisegarver was facing the crowd, pounding his fist on the podium.

"They will not replace us!" his voice thundered, and many of the townspeople applauded. "We will send a petition to the railroad company, demanding that they hire the good men of Manitonka. Otherwise, we won't approve the railroad stop! Otherwise, we'll become overrun with foreigners."

A big man, who had hair the color of harvested corn, raised his hand timidly. When he spoke, Karolina realized he had a Swedish accent.

"Many of us in Manitonka were not born here, Mayor," he said. "One of our schoolteachers is Irish. We have a German brewhouse in the center of town. Some estimate that the city of Manitonka is a fourth Swedish. How can we welcome some newcomers and run others out of town?"

"Swedes like you are of superior European stock," Mayor Wisegarver replied. "Even the mayor of Chicago acknowledges that the Scandinavians are the best immigrants! Their Nordic blood makes them tall and sturdy, primed for working long hours in the outdoors. The Italians are short-statured. Their Mediterranean climate is mild, which makes them prone to laziness. They'll cause nothing but problems for our great town!"

Mayor Wisegarver's wife sat next to him. Now, she rose to speak. She wore a ruffled dress that looked very expensive, and her hair was perfectly arranged in a neat bun.

"Speaking of shifty, we've another problem to address," she said. "All around Manitonka, people's prized possessions are going missing! Just this week, Miss Gustafsson of Maple Avenue lost a porcelain bowl. Another neighbor reported that her beloved Christmas wreath was stolen from her door."

"We're investigating the matter," Mayor Wisegarver said with a smug smile. "But the arrival of foreigners seems to coincide with the disappearance of precious goods."

Some people in the crowd chuckled. Others shook their heads. As the crowd began to disperse, Johan grabbed Karolina's arm.

"We have to get home before Mama and Papa!" he said. The three of them ducked their heads and spirited down Main Street toward home.

On the way, they passed the red boarding house where the Italian railroad workers and their families lived. It sat beside a narrow path worn by wagon wheels. In the darkness, Karolina could see the light of dozens of burning flames.

"Those men are gathering outside the Italians' boarding house with torchlights," Johan said. "That can't be good."

The torchlights illuminated the mens' faces. Even from a distance, Karolina saw that they looked hot and angry. They were chanting something.

"Go home!" they shouted.

For the first time that night, even Johan looked scared. He grabbed his sisters' hands with both of his. "Let's get out of here!" he said.

Johan, Karolina, and Sofia managed to get home and jump into bed just before Mama and Papa. But as she pulled the blankets around her and Sofia, Karolina realized she was still wearing her jacket.

"Oh no!" she said to herself, sitting upright. If Mama saw her coat missing from its peg, she would know something was amiss. Karolina raced downstairs to replace it just as the doorknob turned.

"Karolina! Why haven't you gone to bed yet?" Mama gasped. She was still holding Erik, who slept in her arms.

Karolina began to stammer, unsure of what to say. She couldn't tell her they had

seen everything at the Town Hall meeting. That they saw the mob with torchlights outside the boarding house on Oak Street.

"I was practicing my lesson for tomorrow, Mama," Karolina said. "I have to tell my schoolmates about Christmas in Sweden. About St. Lucia Day."

Mama patted the chair near the fireplace, motioning for Karolina to sit down next to her. "Something is troubling you," she said, "I can see it in your little face."

Karolina frowned, her eyes downcast. She sat down next to Mama, stroking Erik's little blonde head.

"Mama, why don't the townspeople like my new schoolmates?"

"The Italians?" Mama asked. She sighed, looking tired and defeated. "I don't know."

"There must be some reason," Karolina pressed her.

"I suppose some people don't take kindly to strangers," Mama said. "But then again, we were strangers here once. Our people began arriving here in large numbers only a few years ago. They were wary of us, too. But the politicians in Washington told them we were the best immigrants. They say the Scandinavians came from 'good stock.'" Mama laughed a bit. "I'm not sure how they arrived at that notion. I suppose us Swedish folks were lucky."

"What does it mean, anyway?" Karolina asked. "When they say the Italians come from bad stock..."

"It's nonsense. Hogwash, as the Americans call it," Mama replied, and Karolina giggled. "The Italians once ruled the world, you know."

"They did?" Karolina said, her eyes widening. "I thought it was our people who conquered the world."

"Yes, the Scandinavians were fierce warriors and a powerful seafaring people," Mama said. "Many ages ago, they called us the Vikings. We set out in our longboats and we explored the whole continent Europe, sailing the oceans and rivers."

"But the Italians were great men, too. They ruled the ancient world from their Empire in Rome. Do you remember reading about Rome in our Bible, Karolina?" Mama asked.

"Yes!" Karolina replied.

"The Romans were Italians, too, like your new friends at school," Mama said. "They were masters of art and politics, and they built miles of roads and acqueducts. But the Roman Empire fell, and the Italians became poor. Life in Italy is hard, even harder than it was for us in Sweden when the crops began to fail. That's why they want to come to America."

Karolina looked at her stocking feet, poking out below her long nightgown. "I never knew all that," she said.

"Well, the more you learn..." Mama said with a smile. "Do you know who else was from Italy, Karolina?"

"Who?"

"St. Lucia herself," Mama said. "We celebrate her in Sweden, but Lucia was a girl who lived in the Roman Empire in ancient times. She brought food to her fellow Christians who were in prison. They say she wore her candles on her head. That way, she could light her path and still keep her hands free as she carried the food."

Karolina smiled in the glow of the fire crackling in the fireplace. "And that's why we celebrate St. Lucia Day by having a young girl carry a tray of buns, with a wreath of candles on her head!" she said.

"Yes," Mama replied. "Our Swedish celebrations came from Italy. Many things we do come from other places. Do you know what 'Manitonka' means?"

"No," Karolina said.

"Well, the Dakota Sioux Indians' word for 'great' is 'tonka,' and 'mano' is their word for 'bear.' So the name of our town is really Great Bear, Wisconsin."

"I've learned a lot tonight," Karolina said. "Thank you, Mama."

"You are welcome, daughter," Mama said. "Now, go to bed!"

Karolina did go to bed...for a while. But in the middle of the night, she awoke to the sound of an owl hooting in the moonlight. She thought of the thieves roaming Manitonka, stealing porcelain dishes and Christmas wreaths. She hoped nothing would get stolen from her house.

In the middle of the night, Karolina climbed out of the loft and fell asleep before the fireplace. She dreamt of torchlights.

Chapter Four

The next day, Karolina could feel the tension in the schoolhouse as the children took their seats. Some of the students hadn't been kind to their new Italian classmates.

After last night's Town Hall meeting, they walked in with smug smiles of affirmation.

"They're back, eh?" one of the older boys snickered as Natalia and several other children took their seats. "I thought we'd run them out of town by now."

Miss Donahoe overheard, and rapped her ruler on the potbelly stove in the middle of the room. "Quiet," she said. "I hope you've all come prepared for your presentations today. I am aware there was a...disturbance in town last night."

The boys snickered again, and Miss Donahoe's ruler came crashing down on the stove. It sent shockwaves through the whole room.

"Karolina Henriksson, would you like to go first?" Miss Donahoe asked.

Karolina wasn't sure if this was a reward or a punishment. But Miss Donahoe smiled at her as she rose from her seat, calming the steady beat of butterfly wings in her stomach.

Karolina stood at the front of the schoolroom, smoothing her dress with her hands. She remembered to have good posture, as Mama had taught her. Then she sucked in a deep breath.

"I was born in Sweden," Karolina said. "Every year, on the thirteenth of December, Sweden celebrates St. Lucia Day. St. Lucia was a young Christian girl from Italy…"

Some of the students looked at each other. The Italian students recognized the name of their home country. They sat up straighter, giving Karolina their full attention.

"St. Lucia visited other Christians in prison. Legend has it that she wore candles on her head so that she could keep her hands free to deliver food," Karolina said. "That's why, in Sweden, the oldest girl in the family wears a crown of candles, and carries a tray of St. Lucia buns for her family."

Miss Donahoe smiled at her. "And who is the oldest girl in the Henriksson family, Karolina?"

Karolina smiled back. "I am, Miss Donahoe," she said.

At recess that day, Karolina picked some browning grass from the schoolyard and braided a little crown for her doll, Helmi. "St. Lucia Day will be here soon!" she said to Anna and Natalia, who sat on a few old tree stumps beside her. They loved using the tree stumps as chairs during recess.

"It will," Anna said. "And after that, Christmas!"

Natalia made a little mudpie out of the Earth around her feet. She topped it with some red berries they had found in the bushes. Together, Natalia and Karolina pretended to feed Helmi the mudpie cake.

When recess ended, Natalia took Anna and Karolina's hands, so they were joined together in a circle.

"Christmas," Natalia said hesitantly. She motioned toward both of the girls. "With me?"

Anna's face brightened. "Are you inviting us to celebrate Christmas with you, Natalia?" she asked.

Natalia broke into a big smile and nodded. Day by day, she was learning more English.

Chapter Five

A few nights later, before the Henriksson family sat down for supper, Papa added extra logs to the fireplace. It was growing dark earlier every week. Tonight, they could see silvery gusts of snow outside the window.

"Christmas will come soon," Papa said. "It's winter time now. You know the saying: 'From St. Lucia Day, the cold is on its way.'"

"Is St. Lucia Day coming soon?" Sofia asked.

"Yes, Sofia," Mama replied, passing a bowl of milk around the table. "It's only about a week away."

"Why don't we celebrate St. Lucia Day anymore, Mama?" Karolina asked. The question caused Mama to pause and wipe her lips with her cloth napkin.

"When we arrived in America, we decided to do as the Americans do," she said. "I've thought of celebrating it again one year. I suppose I've become too busy to prepare a St. Lucia feast, with cleaning Mr. Wisegarver's home twice weekly. And with the baby." She looked down at Erik, who was sleeping in his cradle.

"What if I made the St. Lucia buns?" Karolina asked.

Mama smiled and passed her the breadbasket. "We'll see," she said. "For now, you must focus on your school work."

Karolina fell asleep easily that night, no longer fretting about thieves. The Henrikssons didn't own many fancy things. Their only valuables were Papa's tools and some china they stored in a painted trunk from Sweden. But Karolina knew the threat wasn't gone. Last night, a friend of Mayor Wisegarver's hosted a dinner for the city council at her home. Her wedding ring went missing after she removed it while washing dishes.

In the middle of the night, Karolina and Sofia awoke to a series of loud knocks on the door.

"Olaf, come quick!" a man's voice said, shouting Papa's name. "There's a fire in town. We need all the water barrels and extra hands we can get!"

Karolina watched Papa bound out of bed, racing to put on his shoes and wool coat. "Where's the fire?" he asked.

"Oak Street."

When Karolina heard Oak Street, she knew in her heart what had happened. She rushed downstairs, searching for her boots. Their neighbor was still waiting in the doorway.

"Stay back, Karolina," Papa said. "It's dangerous out there."

"I have to make sure my friend is alright!" Karolina cried.

"Don't disobey me," Papa said. "It's cold outside, and a burning building is no place for little girls."

Karolina watched some of their neighbors through the window, walking with buckets toward Oak Street. Some teamed up in twos to haul water barrels. When Mama, Johan, and Sofia had gone back to sleep, Karolina laced up her boots and slipped out the door.

When she got to Oak Street, she saw the charred frame of the boarding house. The roof had collapsed. Small pockets of flames were still burning through the windows. Karolina stood in the snow, feeling frozen...and it wasn't just from the frigid winter air.

"What are you doing here, Karolina Henriksson?" a deep voice asked. It was one of her American neighbors, Mr. Barlow. Mr. Barlow wasn't Swedish, but he was a close friend of Papa. He had helped him learn English. He and his family visited once a month for dinner.

"Mr. Barlow, what happened?" Karolina asked.

"It was a terrible fire," he replied. "These poor souls have lost everything they own, and it wasn't much to begin with."

Karolina saw Italian families standing outside the burnt remains of their home. She looked at the mothers holding babies, husbands and wives holding hands. They talked frantically among themselves. A young man, who looked like a railroad worker, sat with his head in his hands and wept.

She didn't see her friend anywhere.

She stepped toward the Italian families, searching among them. "Natalia?" she called, her voice echoing in the night.

No answer.

"Karolina!" Papa's voice thundered. "I told you that you were to go back to bed!"

He whisked Karolina into his strong arms and carried her all the way home. She buried her head in his shoulder, trying to forget the terrible image of the charred remains of the boarding house.

The next day, none of the Italian children came to school. Their absence created an eerie quiet; a chill over the already cold room. Miss Donahoe arrived late, which she never did. She looked pale and weary, but her amber eyes burned like hot embers in a fire.

"Good morning, boys and girls," she said. "As you can see, several of your schoolmates are missing today."

The students sat in stony silence, not daring to speak.

"The boarding house where many of your schoolmates lived caught fire last night," Miss Donahoe continued. "But it wasn't an accident. It was arson. Does anyone know what 'arson' means?"

Jeremiah, an older boy, shot his hand into the air. "Does it mean that the fire was intentional?"

"Yes, Jeremiah," Miss Donahoe replied. "Someone set fire to the building on purpose. They found footprints in the snow, running to and from Main Street. Your schoolmates were left homeless. They are afraid to come to school. Some of the families have packed up and left. But most have no money to return to Chicago, much less to Italy."

"That's not fair," Jeremiah said under his breath.

"What's that, Jeremiah?" Miss Donahoe said.

"It's not fair!" he repeated, louder this time. "They shouldn't have to leave town because someone burnt down their boarding house. It wasn't their fault!"

"You're right, Jeremiah, it's not fair," Miss Donahoe said. "Especially since you have more in common with your schoolmates than you think. Many of you, as well as your mothers and fathers, were born in Sweden. Many of you will celebrate St. Lucia Day next week. Did you know that St. Lucia Day is an important holiday for people in Italy, too?"

"I didn't know that," Karolina's friend, Anna, said.

"It's true," Miss Donahoe said. "In Italy, the people celebrate St. Lucia Day by making special sweet pastries that look like white balls. They call them 'St. Lucia's eyes.' It sounds odd, but they taste delightful. Where I come from, New York, I could buy them at an Italian bakery for a few pennies."

Karolina thought of the time when Natalia created a white ball out of yarn at recess and said, "Lucia." She had been trying to tell her about St. Lucia Day in Italy!

Karolina raised her hand.

"Miss Donahoe," she said urgently, "Do you know where my friend Natalia is staying now?"

Miss Donahoe shook her head. "No, Karolina," she said. "But if I find out, you'll be the first to know."

Chapter Six

The school week ended, and none of the Italian students had returned. When Karolina entered the schoolhouse and saw Natalia's empty seat, her heart filled with sadness. She tried to focus on her lessons, but she found it hard to concentrate.

On Saturday, Mama told Karolina she needed to come with her to Mayor Wisegarver's house. Mayor Wisegarver was having a holiday party for visitors that night. Mama needed an extra set of hands to help clean his big, fancy house.

"I don't want to go to Mayor Wisegarver's house," Karolina protested. "It was his fault that my friend's boarding house burned down!"

From the look in Mama's eyes, Karolina knew she didn't disagree. "Why do you say that, Karolina?" she asked.

"He made the townspeople turn on them," Karolina said. "He told them that if they stayed in Manitonka, they would steal people's jobs. He told people they were from inferior stock. So someone decided to chase them out of town!"

Mama bit her lip. "I know, Karolina," she said. "But for now, I'm still a paid employee of Mayor Wisegarver's, and I have to clean his house."

So Karolina walked with Mama to Mayor Wisegarver's beautiful home in the center of town. Karolina wondered what it would be like to own a house so grand. To be able to cover the dining room table with sparkling white tablecloths and sparkling silverware. Karolina's house didn't even have a dining room. It was built of split logs and had only two rooms: the main room and the loft.

"Hello, Ms. Henriksson," Mrs. Wisegarver said with a stiff smile as Mama and Karolina entered the parlor room. "You didn't inform me you were bringing help today."

"Karolina is swift and thorough with her chores," Mama replied. "We can finish the housework twice as fast."

Mrs. Wisegarver looked displeased. But she nodded.

"Mayor Wisegarver and I will visit the home of a friend while you clean," she said. "I want this whole place spic-and-span for our party this evening. Is that clear, Mrs. Henriksson?"

"Yes, ma'am," Mama said, trying to hide her annoyance. She looked relieved when the Wisegarvers left.

"Karolina, why don't you fetch a fresh tablecloth from the linen closet and put it on the dining room table?" Mama asked. "Mrs.

Wisegarver always wants a new tablecloth when guests arrive."

"Yes, Mama," Karolina said.

She wasn't sure which drawer held Mrs. Wisegarver's collection of ivory tablecloths. First, she opened a bottom compartment, but it was filled with extra bowls and serving platters.

There were rows and rows of drawers.

"The tablecloths must be somewhere," Karolina mumbled to herself. She was careful not to misplace anything, knowing that would make the mayor's wife angry.

Finally, she opened the closet beside the stove. It was stuffed full of random odds and ends, items that didn't match the others in the Wisegarver's house.

There were china dishes, and a Christmas wreath, and a little ring sitting in a serving bowl, where it wouldn't get lost.

"Mrs. Wisegarver!" Karolina gasped. "She must be the one stealing people's things!"

It made sense now. The Wisegarvers were known to call on townspeople regularly as part of Mayor Wisegarver's re-election campaign. Mrs. Wisegarver must be concealing items in her voluminous petticoats, or in the pockets of her fancy coat. Karolina wondered how she had managed to pilfer a Christmas wreath without getting caught.

Karolina scampered into the parlor room, where Mama was dusting the furniture. "Mama, come quickly!" she cried. "Mrs. Wisegarver is the one stealing things from homes in Manitonka!"

Mama's down her duster. "Don't be so excitable, Karolina," she said. "They could just be old items that Mrs. Wisegarver forgot about in an extra closet."

"Impossible," Karolina said. "There's even a ring in there!"

Mama trailed behind Karolina, opening the closet to inspect it for herself. She shook her head in disbelief.

"Don't tell anyone about this," Mama said sternly.

"How could we not tell anyone?" Karolina protested. "Those people need their things back!"

Mama gave Karolina a few pennies, which was what she usually earned for helping clean. "After you set the table, go home," Mama said. "I will take care of this."

On her way home, Karolina made a secret stop at the General Store on Main Street. This place sold basic household items like flour and sugar. She had an idea, one she hadn't shared with anyone else. Not even with Mama, or her sister Sofia, or her best friend, Anna.

She was going to bake *lussekatter,* St. Lucia buns. Swedish people ate lussekatter at St. Lucia Day celebrations every year on December thirteenth. The thirteenth was coming up fast. In fact, if Karolina was counting right, the thirteenth was this Wednesday.

Wednesday was only four days away.

She sidled up to the counter, where a General Store clerk waited on customers.

"I'd like to buy some raisins," Karolina said. She tried her best to sound grown up. "And a sack of flour."

The clerk smiled at her as he took her coins. "Wait right here," he said.

The door to the stock room swung open, and a young boy entered the General Store carrying an armload of goods for the shelf. It was Angelo! Karolina recognized him immediately. Angelo was one of the older Italian boys from school. He was about twelve or thirteen years old, judging from the looks of him. He was one of the few Italian children who spoke some English.

"Angelo!" she cried.

Then her questions came tumbling out.

"Do you remember me? My name is Karolina, and I'm your schoolmate," she said. "Why did you stop coming to school? Do you know where my friend Natalia went?"

He spoke in halting English. His Italian accent was strong and beautiful. He pointed to the swinging stock room door behind him.

"I work here now. We need money. We lost all in the fire."

He looked back at Karolina. "Natalia is a cousin of mine," he said. "We live at the inn on Maple Street."

Karolina felt her spirits sink again. The inn on Main Street was a shabby old hotel. It was in sore need of a new paint job, and its furniture was stained and fading.

"Natalia, she might go to stay with Miss Donahoe," Angelo said. "But that's if we stay in Manitonka at all. This town, they don't want us here."

"Don't go," Karolina begged. "Tell Natalia I must see her one more time. Will she stay until at least December thirteenth?"

Angelo looked at her with sad eyes. He looked tired and worried.

"Yes," he replied. "We will be here."

Chapter Seven

The Day before St. Lucia Day, Karolina told Mama and Papa she had to stay after school to work on a lesson with Miss

Donahoe. She secretly slipped the flour, raisins, and other ingredients she purchased at the General Store into her lunch pail.

After school, she walked to the house where Miss Donahoe boarded. Miss Donahoe was a travelling schoolteacher, so she lived with a family in Manitonka.

"This is a wonderful surprise, Karolina," Miss Donahoe said as she took pots and pans down from their respective hooks above the stove.

"Thank you," Karolina said. But she couldn't help but frown. "Do you think it will go the way we planned?"

Miss Donahoe knelt down to look her in the eye. "I don't know," she said. "We can only hope, can't we?"

It took them a few hours to prepare St. Lucia buns. They rolled them each into an S-shaped bun and sprinkled them with raisins. Miss Donahoe helped Karolina glaze them.

Next, Miss Donahoe showed her how to roll small donuts and sprinkle them with sugar.

"The Italians call these *Occhi di Santa Lucia*," Miss Donahoe said. "It means 'The Eyes of Saint Lucia.' The Italians pray to St. Lucia to protect their eyesight, as do my people, the Irish."

"Can Swedish people pray to St. Lucia to protect their eyes, too?" Karolina asked.

Miss Donahoe laughed. "Of course you can," she replied. "Anyone can."

As the treats were cooling, Miss Donahoe crouched over the chalkboard she had borrowed from the schoolhouse.

"Urgent meeting at the Town Hall," she scrawled in her perfect, lovely handwriting. "Wednesday, December 13, 1882."

She added at the bottom, in big, forceful letters, "Italians Welcome!"

"I'll place this outside the Town Hall tonight, before the men walk to work in the morn," Miss Donahoe said. "Hopefully 'twill not go unnoticed."

Karolina smiled up at her. "It won't," she said. "I'll say a prayer to St. Lucia tonight, just in case."

Karolina was nervous when she went to bed that night, and all day at school the next day. But before recess, Miss Donahoe pulled her aside to reassure her.

Everything will go off without a hitch!" she whispered. "Don't you worry, Karolina. Just don't give away the surprise."

After school, Karolina finally told Mama her secret. Mama broke into a big, warm smile. She hugged Karolina.

"I'm so proud of you," she said. "Come with me. I'll help you get dressed."

Mama opened the painted trunk the Henrikssons had brought all the way from Sweden. Inside was the special St. Lucia Day gown Mama had worn as a young girl.

"I was about your age when I wore it," Mama said. "I bet it will fit you perfect!"

"Miss Donahoe made my wreath," Karolina explained. "I just hope my hair won't catch fire!"

They both laughed.

"It won't," Mama said, "because you'll have the light of St. Lucia to protect you."

When it became dark out, Mama and Karolina met Miss Donahoe at the empty Town Hall. After suppertime, people began to gather outside, looking a little confused.

"There's no one here," Karolina heard a man say from the other side of the door. "Are you sure there's an urgent meeting tonight? The lights are all out!"

As Mama lit the candles in Karolina's wreath, Miss Donahoe took a deep breath and walked toward the door. In one swift move, she threw them open, inviting the confused townspeople to come inside and take seats.

Karolina peaked around the corner. In the semi-darkness, she could see Natalia in her red cloak.

"Come in," Miss Donahoe said, inviting people to fill the rows of bench seats. "I assure you nothing is amiss."

The people sat in the seats and waited. Mama lit the candles perched in Karolina's crown of leaves and berries. Slowly, balancing her tray of St. Lucia buns, she walked into the main room, lighting the path before her.

People smiled and gasped with delight.

They all begin to sing their familiar Christmas carol. Some sang the lyrics in Swedish, while others sang the song in English:

> *Night walks with a heavy step*
> *Round yard and hearth,*
> *As the sun departs from earth,*
> *Shadows are brooding.*
> *There in our dark house,*
> *Walking with lit candles,*
> *Santa Lucia, Santa Lucia!*

When Karolina finished her walk into the Town Hall, people burst into applause.

"Well done!"

"What a beautiful surprise!"

"But that's not all," Miss Donahoe said. "Our new Italian neighbors celebrate Saint Lucia Day, too. We've brought some small toys and gifts for the children, as they do in Italy. We also have *Occhi di Santa Lucia*. Try them—they're delicious!"

Natalia ran up to Karolina and hugged her.

"Natalia!" Karolina exclaimed. "Oh, I thought I might never see you again."

Natalia looked her in the eye. Then, in perfect English, she said, "Merry Christmas, my friend."

"Your English is getting better every day," Karolina said. "I knew it would. I believed in you. You just needed a little practice and someone to share their lesson plans."

Just then, the doors to the Town Hall flew open, and Mayor Wisegarver stormed in. Beside him was his wife, looking huffy.

"I didn't call a meeting," the mayor said. "Who's responsible for this funny business?"

"Thank you for joining us, Mayor," Mama said. "Now that you've arrived, it's time for our second surprise."

She lifted the tablecloth on the small table where Miss Donahoe had placed the St. Lucia buns and *Occhi di Santa Lucia*. Underneath the table were all the items that had been stolen from the people of Manitonka.

"My daughter Karolina found them…in Mrs. Wisegarver's linen closet," Mama said. "I'm glad we are able to return them just in time for Christmas."

Mrs. Wisegarver gasped and clutched her pearl necklace, pretending to be outraged.

"How dare you?" she shouted. "For all we know, you stole them yourself in order to sully my good name!"

Mama didn't flinch. "No," she said. "I find it more plausible that you stole them, in the hopes of pinning it on one of the newcomers in town."

Mrs. Wisegarver stared at her, looking furious.

"But Manitonka is a town that welcomes everyone," Miss Donahoe said. "They welcomed me when I was just a nineteen-year-old schoolteacher from back East. They welcomed the wave of Swedish families that settled here, in search of a new home. And we'll welcome our newest neighbors, also."

Miss Donahoe turned to Mama. "Dagmar, do you want to tell Karolina about *your* surprise for her?"

Mama nodded.

"Yes," she said. "Karolina, you know we have a big, roomy loft in our house, don't we?"

"We do," Karolina agreed.

"While the boarding house is being rebuilt, Natalia and her family will stay with us," Mama said. "It will be like having a new sister, in addition to Sofia. Space will be tight, but I think we can manage. You can help her practice her English every day."

Karolina was so excited she started jumping up and down.

"This is the best Christmas gift ever!" she cried.

"And Christmas is coming soon," Natalia said. Again, she spoke perfect English.

"I'll teach you Christmas carols!" Karolina said. "It's only twelve days away. We can hang our stockings above the fireplace!"

She bit her lip.

"Do you have Christmas stockings in Italy?" she asked. Then she shook her head and smiled. "Never mind. You will this year."

That night, Karolina and Natalia fell asleep side-by-side in the loft, dreaming of sleigh rides and sugar plums.

Made in the USA
Monee, IL
15 December 2021